Big Dog Bonnie

Books About Bonnie:

Big Dog Bonnie • Best Dog Bonnie

Bad Dog Bonnie • Brave Dog Bonnie

Busy Dog Bonnie • Bright Dog Bonnie

Big Dog Bonnie

BEL MOONEY

Illustrated by Sarah McMenemy

WALKER
BOOKS

This is a work of fiction. Names, characters, places and incidents are either the product of the author's imagination or, if real, used fictitiously.

First published 2007 by Walker Books Ltd
87 Vauxhall Walk, London SE11 5HJ

This edition published 2013

2 4 6 8 10 9 7 5 3 1

This book has been typeset in StempelSchneidler

Printed and bound in Great Britain by Clays Ltd, St Ives plc

British Library Cataloguing in Publication Data:
a catalogue record for this book is available from the British Library

ISBN 978-1-4063-5116-3

www.walker.co.uk

For my parents – who love
the real Bonnie
B.M.

To my mother, Gilia
S.M.

Mouse

Ever since he was a very small boy Harry had wanted a dog. Badly.

He used to talk about it all the time: about how everybody ought to have a pet, and more than just a pet, a very special sort of dog – that's what he wanted, no, he *needed* – who'd go with him everywhere, and be his best friend, someone he could talk to, and play games with; and how it was especially important when you were in a new place and didn't know people;

and anyway, dogs were called man's best friend for a very good reason, so that's why life wouldn't be worth living until they had a dog in the family, and—

"Oh, Harry, STOP going on!" his mother said.

"I'll stop when you say I can have a dog. Go on, Mum, for my birthday," he pleaded.

She sighed one of those sighs which came up from her feet all the way through her body, making it limp – so he felt guilty.

"Harry, I've got enough to do without having some great hound galumphing around the house,

knocking things over and making a mess," she said in that voice he knew so well.

It told him that if he went on, it would be his fault if Mum got one of her bad heads and felt upset and tired. It told him that this was hopeless. So he said no more – not that time, anyway. But he knew this would never go away. Because unless he had a dog to call his best friend, he would always be lonely.

Harry sat in his bedroom and talked to his imaginary dog. Prince, he was called – a cross between a Labrador and a collie... No, a German shepherd and a red setter... Well, the truth was, he didn't really know quite what kind of mix the ghost dog was. But he knew Prince was very big, brown-and-black-mixed, with melting chocolate eyes and sharp ears that pricked up at the sound of his name.

Naturally Prince was the cleverest dog in the world. When he stood on his hind legs he was as big as Harry himself, and when he stretched out in front of the TV he looked just like a great big cosy hairy rug. Harry knew he was really a softie, but to the rest of the world he looked like a fearsome guard dog. One bark and any Mean People would just go running. Harry never could quite

decide who these Mean People actually were. Burglars and bullies just about did it, but he also wondered if having a big dog to look after him might stop those big boys in his new school calling him Shorty.

"You're the best dog ever, Princey," he whispered to his ghost-dog friend. Sometimes he'd even reach out his hand and imagine scratching under those soft ears, with that warm doggy smell in his nose. He wanted a dog. He needed a dog. He *ached* for a dog!

"NO!" said Mum for the hundredth time. Or was it the thousandth?

That particular day, school was worse than ever. Harry didn't understand why the others in his class didn't get what it was like to be new, in a strange town, when your mum spent half her time crying about stuff and the other half painting walls, sewing curtains and generally fussing over their new flat. It wasn't that they were mean to him exactly, except for Dave (the toughest, most popular boy in the class) going on about Harry not being able to reach the top shelf in the library. Harry knew that at moments like that his face set into a silly, desperate grin. It said *Just like me, please!* – like when Prince came galloping in from outside all muddy, knowing he was being naughty by making a mess. Then his tongue would loll out and he'd grin, so nobody could be cross for long.

Oh – but there was no Prince.

No dog.

As Harry wandered slowly out of the school gate, he thought how unfair life was.

He didn't see much of Dad because of his new job, new house and new everything else. He watched his classmates rushing ahead of him, some of the girls arm in arm, and wished – wished *so* much – that he could make at least one friend.

Mum looked different today. It wasn't her clothes, although Harry noticed that she looked a bit nicer, in the smart jacket she hadn't worn for ages. No, it was her face. Her cheeks were pink and she even wore a touch of lipstick, while her eyes sparkled in a way he hadn't seen for a long time – not since everything went wrong.

"What's up, Mum?" he asked.

She shrugged her shoulders in an excited way, and beamed at him. "Nothing's up! I've got… Oh, nothing."

As they started to walk home, Harry nudged her. “Come on, Mum! Got what?”

She couldn’t help herself. “A surprise!” she squeaked. “A surprise for you. And for me!”

All the way home an annoying little smile lurked at the corners of her mouth, but she wouldn’t say another word. It wasn’t far to their house, a tall Victorian building divided into flats. They were lucky to have the garden flat, and Mum had already started cutting back and planting, ready for the summer.

When they turned into their road, there was a removals van outside the house next door, which was still one whole home.

"Oh, I hope we get nice neighbours," said Mum absent-mindedly, "and I hope they like my … secret!" She giggled mischievously.

Harry couldn't stand it any more. "Mum!" he almost yelled as she put her key in the door. "TELL ME WHAT THE SURPRISE IS!"

The kitchen door was closed. Mum turned to him with her hand on the doorknob and whispered, "Sweetheart, you've been such a good boy, putting up with everything, and so today I got us a brand new friend. A pet..."

Harry didn't dare to hope. "Is it a kitten?" he breathed.

"No, love, it's what you've always wanted. I got us a dog!"

She threw open the door and Harry ran forward with a little yell of excitement.

"Cool! Come here, boy! But … hey, Mum, where is he?"

He stopped. The kitchen was empty, or so it seemed.

"Look!" said Mum.

And there in the corner by the fridge, sitting up on one of the flowered cushions from the living room, was the smallest, silliest dog Harry had ever seen. It was about the same size as his old teddy; pure white, with floppy ears and tiny black eyes, nose and mouth, like chips of coal in a snowman's face.

When it saw them it wagged an apology for a tail, which curled over its back like a silk whisk. It jumped off the cushion and pitter-pattered towards them on tiny legs, looking excited and afraid at the same time. Mum bent and scooped it up like a baby. The little creature relaxed into her arms.

Harry didn't speak. But that didn't matter, because Mum was chattering away.

"You see, I was passing the RSPCA Cats' and Dogs' Home the other week and something made me go in. I was actually thinking that if we got a kitten you might stop nagging for a dog.

"Anyway, the ladies on the desk were saying that this little one – she's what they call a Maltese – had just been brought in.

You won't believe it, Harry – she'd been left tied to a tree in the park! Who would do such a thing? They reckon she's only six months old. Look at her! No wonder I fell in love. So I said I wanted her if nobody claimed her. I just couldn't help myself – she's *so* sweet. Don't you think she's gorgeous?"

Still Harry couldn't speak.

"They had to come and check where we lived, you know. They go to real trouble to make sure their animals go to good homes. Thank goodness we've got the garden, eh, love? Bonnie's already been out exploring. I think we'll put a cat flap in so she—"

"Bonnie?" he interrupted in a flat voice.

She rattled on. "Yes, love, in the car on the way to get her I was listening to my favourite singer – you know, that one you don't like much, Bonnie Raitt – and it just popped into my mind that this one's a Bonnie too! I know I should have let you choose really, but don't you think it suits her perfectly?"

Harry just stared at the small white dog, and she stared back at him with eyes like black buttons.

For the first time Mum looked closely at him, and started to look worried. "Harry? What's the matter? I thought you'd be excited. Aren't you pleased we've got a dog at last?"

For a couple more minutes Harry was silent. Then he roared, "THAT'S not a dog, Mum – not a PROPER dog!" and rushed from the room before she could see his tears of disappointment.

In his bedroom Harry confided in his big, handsome imaginary friend, whose tongue lolled out in sympathy. "It's just pathetic, Prince – did you see it? More like a stupid little mouse than a dog, and if Mum thinks I'd be seen dead in the street with that thing on a lead, she's wrong! I bet it'd be scared stiff if a cat came into the garden! And *Bonnie*? I mean, what kind of name is *that* to shout out? If Mum wants a girl's dog for herself, that's fine. But that silly little thing's got nothing to do with me! Oh, Princey – I'm *so* fed up..."

At last Mum shouted down the hall that tea was ready. When Harry pushed open the kitchen door, she wore that bright face which said she was upset but determined to make things all right. Bonnie started a shrill yapping which sliced into his brain. "Look, she's saying hello!" smiled Mum as the little dog pranced around.

"Huh. Does she know how to say goodbye?" said Harry.

He sat at the table, and Mum plonked down a plate of shepherd's pie. She was a good cook; it was his favourite. Harry started to feel a bit more cheerful. Bonnie was standing on her hind legs, front paws on his knee, begging to be picked up. She looked quite cute, but Harry thought of Prince and refused to soften. So Mum scooped her up and the little dog snuggled down on her knee as if she'd lived with them for ever.

They ate in silence for a while, then Mum asked, "You do like her *really*, don't you, love?"

"I wanted a dog, not a mouse. She's too *small*."

"Too small for what?"

"Too small for anything!"

"Is she too small to love, Harry?" Mum asked sadly.

At that moment, Bonnie uncurled herself on Mum's knee and sat up, resting her chin on the table. Her bright eyes seemed to look right into Harry's mind; suddenly he felt mean.

"She's all right really," he muttered. "But I'm not taking her out. People will laugh at me."

"Fine," said Mum in her cool voice. "I'll take her for walks myself."

Harry did his homework; Mum watched TV with the dog on her knee, and then insisted he help her search the Internet for dog accessories. "She'll need a pretty bed, and things like that," she said. Harry wanted to scream, and at last he escaped to his room. He read for a while, then Mum came to say goodnight.

"Where's it going to sleep?" he asked.

"In the kitchen," said Mum, giving him a kiss, "and she's not 'it', Harry. She's Bonnie."

She clicked off his light and went out.

Miserable, Harry whispered, "Goodnight, boy," into the darkness, imagining Prince lying down over by his door – always slightly ajar to let some light in. Prince kept him safe; how could a ball of white fluff do that?

Harry didn't know how much later, but he was just slipping into sleep when he heard the tiniest sound, a scraping or scrabbling, as if a mouse was in the skirting board. He raised himself up on one elbow.

Skitter, skitter, skitter across the wooden boards of his room. He imagined a giant spider, or a cockroach… Eeeeuch!

Suddenly he felt a little tugging at his duvet, and glanced down. The small white face seemed to glow in the darkness. Bonnie had her paws up on the side of the bed, and as he stared at her she made a tiny growling noise, as if asking

to be picked up. Without thinking, Harry reached down and lifted her, amazed at how light the dog was in his arms.

"Hello, Mouse-Face," he whispered, "how did you get out of the kitchen? You can't sleep here, you know."

Bonnie put her head on one side and looked at him.

"I mean it," said Harry, putting on his sternest voice.

But the little dog just flopped down, curled into a ball, and went to sleep.

BONNIE was dreaming.

Somewhere in the room, there was an enormous dog. She knew she had met him before: he was very big, brown-and-black-mixed, with melting chocolate eyes and sharp ears that pricked up at the slightest sound. But so did hers. When he began his long low rumbling growl to warn her off, she started up an answering one in her own throat: a fierce sound that would strike terror into the heart of any rat.

Oh, she'd grab it, shake it, finish it off all right! And just because he was a big dog, not a rat, it didn't mean she wouldn't see him off too.

Grrrrr, on your way! I'll yap up such a storm you won't know what's hit you. There's only room enough for one dog in this home.

Rabbit

Harry was so amazed to wake to find a small white bundle curled up in the crook of his legs, he found himself grinning without knowing it – and completely forgot to say hello to Prince.

It was Saturday. Usually he liked to stay in bed, sleeping or daydreaming, until Mum came and told him they had to go to the shops or tidy up or do something equally boring. But today he jumped out of bed and pulled his clothes on. Bonnie sat up watching, head on one side and pink tongue protruding slightly. She looked just like a soft toy and this made him grin all the more.

She moved to the edge of the bed, looked down at the floor, then looked at Harry again. He thought how impossibly small she was.

"Aha – you can't jump, can you, Mouse-Face? It's too high for your silly short legs – so what are you going to do?"

Feeling just a little bit mean, he moved towards his bedroom door, pretending to leave her. But when he looked back Bonnie was taking a flying leap. She landed with a clatter on the shiny floor, then trotted

after him as if nothing had happened. Her tail curled cheekily over her back.

Mum glanced up from her newspaper and smiled broadly. She pointed to the empty cushion on the floor. "What have you two been up to? Didn't take up too much room on your bed then, Harry?"

"I didn't ask her to come in," he mumbled.

"Don't try and sound grumpy!" Mum laughed. "You loved it!"

Harry said nothing. To tell the truth, he had woken in the middle of the night, felt the unexpected bundle by his leg, reached down to see what it was – and then settled back with a sigh when his fingers met the soft, warm body. It had felt so comforting, just as if the old teddy he used to cuddle (who now lived on the chest of drawers so his stuffing wouldn't come out) had come alive and was breathing there in the darkness, keeping him company. Instead of lying awake and worrying – about school and Dad and whether Mum was lonely and if he would ever meet Prince in real life – Harry had just turned over and gone straight back to sleep.

"I think you should start training Bonnie," Mum said when they'd finished breakfast. "Teach her to sit, things like that. Take her into the garden while I wash up."

"Mu–um!" Harry protested. "She won't be able to learn anything. Her brain must be the size of a peanut."

Bonnie looked up at him reproachfully.

"I don't know," murmured Mum, picking the dog up and stroking her head. "Maybe a walnut?"

Harry gave a snort of disgust and stomped out of the room, not noticing that Bonnie trotted after him, as if tied to his ankle by an invisible cord.

It was cold but sunny. The flower beds were starred with daffodils, and clumps of snowdrops glimmered under the trees. Bonnie scampered over the grass, then turned to face him, giving a little yip and crouching back over her hind legs.
She lifted up one front paw and stamped it down, giving another yap.

Harry stared at her.

"If you think I'm going to play with you, you're so wrong," he said, and turned away.

But the dog took no notice. She ran around in front of him and did the same thing, stamping twice this time. She looked funny, but Harry wouldn't allow himself to smile.

"Bonnie – come!" shouted Mum from the back door, and to Harry's amazement the new member of the family darted off and jumped up against Mum's leg.

"How did you teach her that?" he asked.

"I didn't! Girls don't need teaching, do they, Bonnie?" said Mum with a knowing wink.

Then she told Harry news that made him feel excited and nervous all at once. The house next door had been empty for a while, then builders had been coming and going, and yesterday they had seen a removals van at the door. "And this morning I saw the parents," said Mum, "and there's two children! They look your age, so maybe you'll make some new friends,

Harry. Wouldn't that be lovely? I hope we get on with them. Maybe I'll pop round—"

"No!" shouted Harry.

"But it's nice to be friendly, love."

Harry imagined the family being rich and stuck up; after all, they'd bought the whole enormous house, while Harry and his mum were just in a two-bedroom flat.

He imagined them pretending to be friendly with Mum but laughing at her behind her back, not really wanting to be friends at all. And he couldn't bear it.

"Let them move in first," he said in his grumpiest voice. "They don't want *you* fussing over them."

His reward was the hurt look on Mum's face as she bent quickly to pick up the dog. They disappeared, leaving Harry alone in the cold garden.

It felt lonely. He kicked at the grass, wondering where his good mood had gone,

and why. He could hear music coming from the house next door, and as he looked up at the windows thought he saw a dark head move quickly back. But he couldn't be sure. He started to worry again. If the children were his age, how would he get to know them? What if they were really horrible? Would that be worse than if they were great, but didn't want to be friends? What if they had millions of friends already and thought he was boring? What if they had a really scary dog with big teeth like a wolf, and he ate Bonnie?

Be a good thing, he said to himself, but he knew he didn't mean it.

How did you get to know people?

How did you make friends?

Harry sighed. He wasn't doing so well in this new town.

After he'd watched some Saturday morning TV, and eaten an apple, and glared at Mum because she insisted on carrying the silly dog around like a baby, Harry drifted out into the garden again. He half thought he might pick some daffodils to say sorry to Mum, then looked around and decided there weren't enough. He tried not to stare up at the house next door, but he couldn't help wondering what the new neighbours were doing.

He looked down. Bonnie was at his heels. Despite himself he smiled when he saw her. She had to be the smallest dog in the world, and there was something so funny about the way she looked up at him as if to say, "Don't be boring! Play with me!" But Harry had never had a real dog and somehow he knew this wasn't the kind that ran after a stick. So just what *did* she do?

Immediately, as if Bonnie could read his mind, she set up the noisiest yapping he had ever heard. She ran over to the tall fence which separated them from the house next door and stood glaring at it, making the terrible noise. Her back legs were splayed out as if she was squaring up to an invisible enemy. Then she jumped up against the fence shrieking, "YIP YIP YIP YIP YIP YIP YIP" ... without stopping.

It was as if she was threatening something she knew was there, even though she couldn't see it.

Or somebody.

A cloud passed over the watery spring sun, making Harry shiver. "Is there anyone there?" he shouted at the fence.

Nobody spoke, but Bonnie carried on barking, dancing on the spot, and spinning round and round, getting crosser by the minute.

There was quite a wide crack above her that Harry had never noticed. He crept forward and narrowed his eyes. Could it be? Surely he was imagining things. But no – as the little dog twisted and yipped and turned and yapped, Harry realized he was staring straight at somebody's eye.

"Hey!" he said.

"Hi," said a boy's voice.

Harry heard a noise, as if something was being moved, and then a muffled giggle – which sounded like a girl – and a few minutes later a boy's head appeared over the fence. He looked a bit older than Harry, and stared down with cool confidence.

"What on earth's *that*? It's very noisy."

Harry cringed. He opened his mouth to speak but the boy didn't wait. "It's smaller than our rabbit!" he said with a broad grin. It wasn't said in a nasty way, but as if they were sharing a joke.

"Louder voice, though!" said Harry with an answering grin.

"What's your name?"

"Harry. And this is Bonnie. She's a dog, believe it or not."

"I'm Zack Wilson. And this is my sister, Zena. We're twins, see. Though you wouldn't think it if you saw her try and catch a ball."

He jerked a thumb over his shoulder, then said "Ouch!" as the unseen sister whacked him. There was a scuffle, laughter, and Zack disappeared. Seconds later a different head was looking over the fence. Zack's hair was cropped into little gelled tufts; Zena's was long and straight, a shiny, dark brown curtain she tossed back as she smiled down. But not at Harry.

"Oh, I just love your tiny dog!" she squealed.

Bonnie yapped.

"She's so *cute*! What's her name?"

"Er … Bonnie," said Harry, feeling himself go red.

He bent down swiftly and scooped Bonnie up, shushing her and holding her tight. She fell silent right away.

"Oh, she's lovely! And so clever! She does just what you say," cried Zena, beaming at them both.

"Uh … y-yeah, she does – and I'm going to start training her soon," said Harry, trying to sound cool, and realizing he liked the feel of Bonnie in his arms.

"It's a rabbit!" came Zack's voice.

"No, *smaller* than a rabbit!" Harry shouted back, and Zena burst out laughing.

"Can I come round and play with her?" she asked.

It was as easy as that. Within five minutes the doorbell rang, and Harry's mum was astonished to find two strange children on the doorstep.

"We've come to see Bonnie," said Zena in a clear voice.

They ate biscuits, and Zena chased Bonnie around the garden, then Harry showed them his room and was glad when they said his posters were cool. They told him they'd moved from the other side of town because their parents had fallen in love with the bigger house, but Zena said she preferred Harry's flat, because it was much cosier. And all the time Bonnie ran around, sometimes deciding these two were the enemy again and yapping at them like mad.

"She's a good guard dog," said Zena.

"Guard rabbit!" said Zack.

Harry laughed.

At last they went home, promising that Harry could come and see their house once the boxes were unpacked. And Zena told Harry's mother that her mother would love to meet her, so Harry's mum said she would invite them round for a cup of tea in a couple of days' time; and everybody said goodbye, feeling pleased. Bonnie had made friends with Zena but still barked at Zack, so that was the last sound the Wilson twins heard as the door closed behind them.

"Well, Rabbit, do you ever stop?" asked Harry, picking Bonnie up. She was silent right away, and flopped her little head down on his arm as if she was tired.

"Not surprising, all that noise you've been making," he said softly.

Mum put the television on and they cuddled up on the sofa, with Bonnie in the middle.

"Well, sweetheart, looks like you've made some new friends."

"Yep," said Harry happily.

"You never told me how you got talking to them," she asked lazily, reaching out to ruffle his hair.

Harry grinned, looked down, and ruffled Bonnie in turn. Then he took hold of her long floppy ears and held them up straight above her head.

"It was easy," he said. "The rabbit introduced us."

Bonnie felt the warmth
from both of them wrap round her
as she snuggled down, feeling sleepy
again. What a hard-working day!
It was all right now the strangers had gone,
but she would have to be careful.
These two would let anybody into their home!
Bonnie knew her job was to look after her pack,
even though they walked on two legs not four,
and the first thing to do was knock them
into shape. She'd start by doing everything
they asked – all that sitting and staying and
coming stuff – because that way they'd think
they were in charge.

But how could they be – when they
were both so little?

FOX

Harry was in the school library. He liked books about animals, though he'd stopped reading *The Big Book of Dogs*, because what was the point of a big book when you'd been unlucky enough to land the tiniest dog on the planet? He'd sneaked a look at the Maltese page and been horrified to see a primped white toy with silky hair and ears streaming right down to the ground like a long dress, topped off with – horror! – a pink bow in its hair. He'd shut the book with a snap. Is that what she'd grow into? How would he live it down?

Harry was fed up. How was it you could be in a building full of people and feel so alone? Two of the bigger boys had pushed past him in the corridor shouting, "Out of the way, squib!" It had made him feel bad, but Harry knew he just had to grin and pretend he didn't care. I wish I was miles and miles away, he thought.

That was what made him pull out a book with polar bears on the cover. Harry liked his mum's stories about sledging when she was a girl, when the snow drifted deep and she always made a snowman.

"Bonnie's face reminds me of that," she would laugh, "except her nose isn't like a carrot!"

Harry flicked the book open – and stared. The beautiful colour picture made him smile. Curled up in the snow – as cosy as if it were a duvet – was a white ball of fluff with coal-black eyes and a small pointy black nose. He read:

The Arctic fox is at home in the snow and ice of the Arctic. It is the size of a large cat and just as agile – standing on its hind legs and jumping up straight in the air when it needs to. It is white and fluffy with a curling tail and sharp claws. The snow fox is a friendly little creature with a big personality.

"Just like Bonnie," said Harry aloud.

Bonnie sometimes stood on her hind legs and danced about, paws in the air, especially if you held up a dog treat.

Suddenly he felt cheered up.

He looked at pictures of polar bears, seals and wolves, and the Inuit people; then told Mrs Smith, the librarian, that he wanted to borrow the book. She smiled and said, "Are you planning a trip to the North Pole, Harry?"

"One day!" he replied with a grin, tucking the book under his arm and feeling pleased that she'd remembered his name.

"By the way," she added, "who's Bonnie? I overheard you."

"Oh, she's my – I mean, my mum's dog," he said. "She looks a bit like a snow fox, only smaller."

That afternoon, Mr Mount said they were going to write about a job they'd like to do when they grew up, but first they'd talk about it all together. "And please don't just say the first thing that comes into your head – like being a famous footballer," said the teacher.

Usually Harry felt too shy to join in; any ideas in his brain seemed to go running away, leaving him facing the world by himself.

Today was different. He put up his hand.

"I'd like to be a polar explorer," he said.

The others looked interested.

When Mr Mount asked him why, Harry told them how he wanted to go and see the way the animals lived, even though it was cold and dark for so much of the year. With all the pictures from the book in his head, he had lots to say. He said he was especially interested in the snow fox – and polar bears too.

"Well done, Harry, that's a really good one," said Mr Mount, and three or four of his classmates nodded at him as if to agree. Harry felt ten feet tall.

🐾 🐾 🐾

They'd had Bonnie for over a week now, and Harry had just about got used to seeing Mum waiting outside school with the small white dog on a black velvet lead. Most days one or two of the boys pointed and laughed, while the girls cooed, "Oh, she's so *cute*!" – which made Harry feel even more embarrassed, and want to hurry away.

Today Bonnie went mad when she saw him, leaping up against his legs, begging to be picked up. And suddenly Harry realized that it was sort of through the dog that his day had been a success for a change. Bonnie was the snow fox.

He bent down to scoop her up. Wriggling like mad, paws flailing in different directions, she licked him wildly all over his face, making him duck and squirm.

"Yuck – dog lick!" he yelled.

"Aaaah, so sweet! She really loves you!" called out a couple of passing girls. Harry laughed as he realized that everybody who was looking at them wore a smile. Even the bigger boys.

That – as Mum said later – was the Bonnie effect.

Back at home Mum handed Harry an envelope. He recognized Dad's writing and his tummy gave a little flip. He always loved hearing from his dad, yet hated it too.

It made him think about sad and happy things at once and that made him spin around – just like Bonnie when she heard the doorbell.

He opened the card, which had a picture of a steamship on the front. The note was short and Dad's writing big because he didn't have much to say. Just that his new job meant he wouldn't be able to see Harry at the weekend, and not for three more, but he was sorry and they'd have a great time when they did get together. He enclosed a ten-pound note.

Without realizing what he was doing, Harry let out a low groan.

"Yip yip yip," said Bonnie for no reason.

Harry tucked the money in his trouser pocket, aimed the card at the waste-paper basket, and went to join Mum in the kitchen.

She looked at him, but said nothing.

Harry took a biscuit and stuffed it whole into his mouth so he couldn't talk, even if she asked him.

There was a silence.

Then: "Grrrrr-rrrrrrr … grrrrr."

Bonnie rushed into the room with something gripped between her teeth, shaking it around as if she'd caught a rat and growling that funny muffled growl. When Harry bent down to try to get whatever she'd found, Bonnie whizzed round on the spot and scampered away. He was always amazed she could move so fast.

"Grrrrrrr-rrrrrr."

Bonnie was over by the sink now, right by Mum – who bent quickly with a sharp "Give it here!" then said, "Good girl."

She held up the mangled paper. Harry glimpsed a picture of a steamship. Mum read the card, then held it out with a sad smile.

"Where did she get this?"

"Out of the bin – unless I missed."

"Ah," she said, "Bonnie thought I ought to know about it, didn't she?"

Harry nodded.

"She's a bright dog," said Mum.

"Yes, she is," he said, taking the crumpled card and tucking it into his pocket with the money.

"We'll do something nice on Saturday instead," was all Mum said.

She was happier these days. She said it was because she liked having company during the day. "Bonnie follows me everywhere." Harry liked the way Mum would sometimes

sit down now instead of always fussing and doing jobs with a sigh, just because she liked to cuddle their new pet on her knee.

Foxes were supposed to be clever, weren't they? Yes, thought Harry, she's a very smart little fox indeed.

It was raining on Saturday, but Mum said it didn't matter. It wouldn't spoil her plan. "We're going on a little outing," she smiled.

Harry felt excited, and forgot to think about Dad. He watched TV, did some homework, and stared at the clock without knowing why. At last the doorbell rang and Bonnie yelped, spun round and round, and threw herself against the door. Harry opened it to see Zack and Zena standing there.

"Surprise!" Zena said.

"I love pizza," said Zack.

"I thought we'd go out for lunch for a change," Mum explained. "Everybody needs a treat once in a while – and I thought it would be nice for these two to come with us. On a gloomy old day like today, what we all need is pizza – and ice cream."

"Cool!" said Harry, trying to stop the grin from splitting his face.

"What are we celebrating?" asked Zena.

Harry thought quickly. "We've had Bonnie for … er … two weeks!"

They piled into the car and drove to the pizza restaurant. Harry clutched Bonnie on his knee in the front. Zack and Zena were in the back, chatting away as if they'd known him for years.

When Mum had parked the car they wandered over to the pizza place – then Harry stopped.

"Look!" he groaned.

"Oh no!" said Zena.

"That's rubbish!" shouted Zack.

The sign on the door showed a black dog (which looked a bit like Harry's old imaginary friend Prince), but with a red line through him.

"No dogs," groaned Mum.

"Can we leave her in the car?" Zack suggested. "It's not sunny, and it won't be for that long."

"No," said Harry, "I read in the paper that people steal dogs. They could smash the window and take her."

As he said that he shivered. He realized just how terrible that would be. Life without their tiny white dog? Impossible!

Suddenly Mum beamed. "I've got the most brilliant idea," she whispered. "But first I have to have a very serious talk with Bonnie. I think it'd be best if you three go in – say I'm just coming – and get a table for four."

"But what about—" Harry began.

"Shh!" said Mum.

A few moments later, the children were sitting at the table by the window when Mum marched in. The pockets of her coat bulged oddly, her big brown leather bag was slung over her shoulder, and she was resting one hand on it. There was no sign of Bonnie.

She sat down on the bench seat beside Harry and winked at him.

"Well, gang – have you chosen your pizzas?" she asked in a loud voice.

Harry stared at her, and saw her eyes flick down to the bag on the bench between them. Zack and Zena were looking at the menu. Nobody said anything.

Soon they were munching slices of pizza, and all three children knew just how clever Mum had been.

"I had to think of something," she said, "but I had to tell her firmly that she mustn't make a sound. Honestly, Bonnie's so bright she obviously understood every word I said." The zip of her bag was open at one end and when he knew nobody was watching, Harry sneaked his hand in to stroke the soft warm body curled up at the bottom. Mum had stuffed all her bits and pieces in her pockets so there was plenty of room for the tiny dog. Bonnie was snug and contented.

Nobody knew she was there – and they all ate great pizza, followed by chocolate and vanilla ice cream.

"Did you all enjoy yourselves?" asked the waitress as she picked up the money.

"Yes, thanks – ALL of us," smiled Mum.

"Could we have this leftover slice in a doggy bag?" asked Harry innocently, and the twins collapsed with giggles.

That night Harry was sitting happily reading the book about the Arctic. Mum was singing in the kitchen as she rattled pots and pans. Bonnie lay beside him, her chin resting on the edge of the chair cushion. It always made him feel quietly content just to know she was there.

He turned to the pages on the snow fox once more. He saw how its coat changes from grey-brown in the summer to white in the winter, so it won't be seen in the snow.

Smart.

He learned how it digs down to the coldest layer of ice to hide its food, storing it for winter shortages – just like putting it in the freezer.

Clever.

He read how a snow fox will often follow a polar bear, to chew on its leftovers. But since polar bears think of snow foxes as a tasty snack, it has to be very cunning to avoid becoming the polar bear's lunch.

Brave.

Harry thought of everything Bonnie did to make them love her – and suddenly realized that this was about survival too. He picked her up – so light, she was – and held her in front of his face, gazing into her jet-black button eyes.

"Who'd have thought one small dog could really be such a clever little fox?"

Bonnie sat under the table.

They were in the kitchen, making all those happy sounds she couldn't always understand, except when she heard her own name – which was very often. And she'd started to recognize "Sit" and "Stay" and "Come here!" too, especially as Harry gave her a tasty bite to eat each time she obeyed. "Good boy" she said to him in her head as he gave her what she wanted. It was so easy to make him happy.

Bonnie watched as Harry's mum washed out her bowl, then Harry spooned food into it. It smelled good – better than that stuff they'd been eating when she was inside the handbag. Chicken and turkey flavour, she guessed, licking her lips. Not bad at all. And how clever my little pack is to hunt it down for me. But of course they have to. Because they know I'm the leader.

5

Bear

One sunny day Harry put Bonnie on her lead and walked next door to see Zack and Zena. They were all good friends now. Harry was happier than he had ever been – and even liked school much more. He dated it all back to when Bonnie came to stay. That's why he felt guilty when, in his heart, he still wished he had a big dog.

Once, in the street, a scruffy man with a fierce-looking dog on a piece of string had shouted at him and Mum, "That's not a dog, it's a rat on a lead!"

Mum had gone red and clamped her lips together. "Cheek!" she'd muttered when they were safely on their way.

Another time a teenage boy had yelled, "Watch out a cat doesn't get it!" and made his friends laugh.

"It's not fair really," Harry explained to Zena. "I mean, they don't *know* her."

"Lovely presents come in small parcels," she said.

"Inside Bonnie there's an enormous dog trying to break out!" said Zack.

"Yes, maybe she thinks she *is* big," Harry said thoughtfully.

Then they rushed out into the garden, where Bonnie was crouched down, yapping furiously at the Wilsons' rabbit in his hutch. The huge black and white rabbit munched peacefully at a pile of lettuce leaves.

"Look – Major isn't a bit scared," laughed Zena.

"That's cos he knows he's bigger!" said Zack.

There was no getting away from it, thought Harry glumly. Bonnie really was a very, very silly dog. When people asked if she would get any bigger, Mum usually replied, “No, what you see is what we’ve got!”

Sometimes an old lady would smile and say, “And how old is your sweet little puppy, my love?” and Harry would have to grunt that the dog was fully grown.

“Really?” she’d say, with a twinkle.

Really.

Harry was playing a computer game with Zack, while Zena sat Bonnie on her knee to watch. But Bonnie didn’t like the noises and began to shake.

“What’s wrong with her?” Zena asked.

"Oh, she gets scared of all kinds of stuff. I mean, she shivers when Mum has to leave her alone in the house for an hour."

"Scaredy-dog!" said Zack, and Harry joined in the laughter. But he knew he shouldn't. He ought to stick up for Bonnie, because you always stick up for your friends. And Bonnie was his friend. No doubt about that.

Today was going to be fun. Mr and Mrs Wilson had invited Harry and his mum – and Bonnie – to join them and some friends for a picnic on Belvedere Common. Harry knew his mum had started getting ready early because she felt quite shy and nervous. It was simple. The Wilsons had much more money than they did, and Mrs Wilson was very young and cool. They were warm, kind and friendly, but very different from the people Harry and his mum used to know in their old town.

Simon Wilson owned a huge four-wheel drive, with plenty of room for all of them. He tossed bags of food and a heavy cooler into the boot, then invited Harry's mum to jump in the front next to him. She went pink and Harry smiled to himself. Rosie Wilson got in the back with the three children and Bonnie, and soon they were bowling along, the windows wide open. Bonnie stood on Harry's lap on her hind legs, her paws on the window edge, her ears blowing in the wind.

Another family was already waiting in the car park: two grown-ups, a toddler and a boy Harry's age. "He's my best mate, Jonno," explained Zack as they rolled up and parked. Harry felt an odd twist in his tummy when he heard that, but smiled all the same.

Simon Wilson introduced everybody. Their friends were Peter and Maggy Brown, with Jonno and little Maisie – who squealed with delight when she saw Bonnie, and tried to grab one of her ears with a sticky hand.

"Wabbit!" she said.

"No, she's a tiny doggy," smiled Harry's mum.

"Wabbit – want wabbit!" yelled the little girl, grabbing the dog's ears and tugging them up straight.

Poor Bonnie looked terrified, and everybody started to laugh.

Harry didn't like that much. And he didn't like it when Zack and Jonno started mucking about like people do who've known each other for a long time, rushing ahead carrying picnic rugs and putting them over their heads pretending to be ghosts. He heard Rosie Wilson tell his mum that the Browns had been their friends back at college, which was why they all knew each other so well. Zena was walking along holding Maisie's hand and smiling down as the little girl chattered away. They were all getting on so well – and Harry felt left out.

He let Bonnie pull him ahead on the long lead. She snuffled into every tussock of grass and chased leaves, and sometimes snapped at something that wasn't there. As usual the sight of her funny, fluffy rear end and silly white flag of a tail made Harry smile. He couldn't help it. It was the Bonnie effect.

Soon they reached the picnic place with wooden tables scattered under the trees. As the grown-ups settled down, Zack pulled a frisbee from one of the bags and rushed off with Jonno to play. They didn't ask Harry. He knew it was just because they

were excited to see each other again, but it made him feel bad inside.

"Shall we go and join in?" asked Zena.

He nodded.

"Why don't you let Bonnie off the lead so she can play too?" she added.

Harry looked around. This was safe. There were no roads, no traffic, no signs warning you to keep your dog on a lead. He looked over at his mum and was pleased to see that she was sipping a plastic glass of white wine and chatting to the other two women as if she had known them for ever.

With Bonnie at their heels, Harry and Zena ran over to where Zack and Jonno were throwing the frisbee.

"Over here!" Harry called, but Jonno threw to Zena.

Then, when Zack threw to him, it was far too high and though Harry jumped into the air he missed, and the frisbee went spinning into a thick clump of bushes. He heard Jonno laugh. It wasn't fair.

Then Bonnie was in the thicket ahead of them all,

rootling and
rustling, scraping
and scratching. Jonno
stood with his hands
on his hips and said,
"What we need here is a
proper dog – like a retriever. That overgrown
hamster won't be able to pick up a frisbee!"

Bonnie, fetch it, girl! Fetch it! Harry pleaded
inside his head.

And within minutes, out she trotted, the
yellow frisbee clamped in her mouth
even though it was four times
the size of her head.

Zack, Zena and
Harry all clapped
their hands,
while Jonno
looked amazed.

"All *right*!" he shouted.
"The wabbit bites back!"

They were hungry. It was time for chicken legs, sandwiches, quiche, cheese, fruit, and the other delicious things the Wilsons had brought. They all piled in. The adults drank white wine, and the children had apple juice. It was a great picnic – but then Jonno spoiled it again.

He picked Bonnie up with one hand and laughed out loud. "Look," he said, "one hand! She'd blow away in a big wind!"

Harry glared at him.

"Aren't we allowed to tease you about your … er … dog?" smirked Jonno.

"No," Harry said. "You're not."

"Good for you, Harry!" said Zena.

"When you think about it," added Harry's mum gently, "you don't say a wren isn't a bird just because it's small, do you? It's as much of a bird as a magpie, or even an eagle. Just different."

"Good point," said Mr Wilson.

"Right!" said Harry, folding his arms.

They all went on talking, sitting around one of the rustic tables. Bored, little Maisie got down and wandered around on the grass near by. She saw some buttercups a little way off and decided to go and take a look. The sun was shining; it was very peaceful. Maisie ambled further away.

Then suddenly there was the most terrible sound – like a wild animal about to attack. From behind a clump of trees raced an enormous brown hound, chased by a young man waving a lead in one hand and a muzzle in the other.

"Come here, Rex!" he yelled. "Come back NOW!"

The dog stopped for a moment, then saw Maisie and let out a dreadful snarl. He changed direction and raced towards the toddler.

It was only then that the grown-ups at the table saw what was happening, and Mrs Brown gave a small, sharp scream.

But Maisie was a long way away and the dog was too fast.

Then a tiny white bundle, jet-propelled, was racing between the giant dog and the little girl. Bonnie's yapping was ear-splitting.

She squared herself, back legs out as if she was about to leap, and challenged the other dog – who stopped dead in his tracks, frozen with shock, his mouth open to reveal a lolling tongue and huge, scary teeth.

Rex looked stunned. He had never seen anything like Bonnie. He knew she was a dog – because she smelled like a dog and sounded like a dog – yet she didn't look like any dog he had ever seen, and he was confused.

"Wow-wow-ow-ow-ow-ow-ow," yelped Bonnie.

Then she gave her best, low, blood-curdling *Grrrrrrrrrrr.*

Maisie started to cry, but by now the young man had run up, puffing, and grabbed hold of his dog's collar. Mr Brown raced to lift his daughter into the safety of his arms.

"You shouldn't let a dog like that off the lead!" he shouted.

"I know – I'm sorry. It was just for a minute, but then he ran off," said the big dog's owner apologetically.

"Oh my goodness!" cried Mrs Brown tearfully, taking Maisie from her father.

The young man quickly led Rex away, and everybody just stared at Bonnie, who was begging for Harry to pick her up.

"Wow!" said Zack. "*Super*-Wabbit."

"She's so brave!" said Zena.

"Brave as a bear," said Mr Brown.

"She's the coolest, bravest dog I've ever seen," said Jonno, still looking a bit shocked. "She saved my little sis."

"Oh, I'm *so* grateful," said Mrs Brown, her eyes wet.

Harry had never felt so proud in his life. Cuddling Bonnie close, he turned back towards the picnic table. He couldn't speak. Suppose the big dog had attacked her? Suppose … no, he didn't want to think about that. All that mattered was that Bonnie had been brave – and now nobody would ever say she wasn't a proper dog.

"Give her some chicken, love," said his mum, looking as proud as he felt.

"Let me chop it up," offered Mrs Wilson.

Everybody fussed over Bonnie, and Jonno

invited Harry to bring her on a visit to his house, with Zack and Zena, as soon as possible.

"Little Bear and I will think about it," grinned Harry, trying not to sound too pleased.

"Why d'you think she wasn't scared of that huge dog?" asked Mr Wilson at last.

"These small dogs can be very protective of their owners," explained Harry's mum, "and so they can actually get quite fierce."

"That Rex didn't know what to think!" laughed Zack.

"There's only one thing to think," said Harry proudly. "Inside Bonnie's little body there's a very big dog – one who can take on the whole world."

"Yep. Yep yep yep!" agreed Bonnie. And everybody laughed with her.

It was the middle of the night. Harry was fast asleep, one arm flung out to touch Bonnie, who was curled in a tight ball. Before putting out the light they'd played Scratch the Bedclothes for ages, Bonnie leaping about like a mad thing. At last Harry had whispered, "Goodnight, Little Bear," and they'd gone to sleep. But not for long.

Bonnie opened her eyes and stared into the darkness. She thought about that big dog, and how she'd seen him off, and wondered why all the people had made such a fuss. That chicken was good, though ... mmm... She licked her lips at the memory.

She pricked up her ears. The old house creaked and shifted in the cool of the night. Harry's arm was too heavy. She wriggled free and went to stand on the edge of the bed, listening. What was there? A big dog who might hurt Harry?

She'd see it off! She'd frighten a burglar! She'd sort out Mean People! She'd bark at the dark!

But there was nothing there.

Still Bonnie stood guard. She knew her job was to protect her pack – for ever. So she couldn't be too careful.

Light from the door threw her shadow across the shiny wooden floor of Harry's room.

And Bonnie saw how huge she was, and how scary.

Love Bonnie? Then why not read all six of her tail-wagging adventures!

To find out more about the books and the real-life Bonnie who inspired them, visit belmooney.co.uk

Bel Mooney is a well-known journalist and author of many books for adults and children, including the hugely popular Kitty series. She lives in Bath with her husband and real-life Maltese dog, Bonnie, who is the inspiration for this series. Bel says of the real Bonnie: "She makes me laugh and transforms my life with her intelligence, courage and affection. And I just know she's going to pick out a really good card for my birthday."

Find out more about Bel at belmooney.co.uk

Sarah McMenemy is a highly respected artist who illustrates for magazines and newspapers and has worked on diverse commissions all over the world, including art for the London Underground, CD covers and stationery. She illustrated the bestselling City Skylines series and is the creator of the picture books *Waggle* and *Jack's New Boat*.
She lives in London.

Find out more about Sarah at sarahmcmenemy.com